FAMOUS FIVE

SHORT STORIES

WHEN TIMMY
CHASED THE
CAT!

The Famous Five

Timmy   Anne   Dick   Julian   George

Text copyright © Hodder & Stoughton Ltd, 1956
Illustrations copyright © Hodder & Stoughton Ltd, 2014

Enid Blyton's signature is a registered trade mark of Hodder & Stoughton Ltd

Text first published in Great Britain in Enid Blyton's Magazine Annual – No. 3, in 1956.
Also available in The Famous Five Short Stories, published by Hodder Children's Books.
First published in Great Britain in this edition in 2014 by Hodder Children's Books

The rights of Enid Blyton and Jamie Littler to be identified as the Author
and Illustrator of the Work respectively have been asserted by them in
accordance with the Copyright, Designs and Patents Act 1988

2

A Catalogue record for this book is available from the British Library
ISBN 978-1-444-91628-7
Printed in China
Hodder Children's Books
A division of Hachette Children's Books
Hachette UK Limited, 338 Euston Road, London NW1 3BH

www.hachette.co.uk

Enid Blyton

WHEN TIMMY CHASED THE CAT!

illustrated by **Jamie Littler**

Hodder
Children's
Books

A division of Hachette Children's Books

Famous Five Colour Reads

For a complete list of the full-length
Famous Five adventures, turn to
the last page of this book

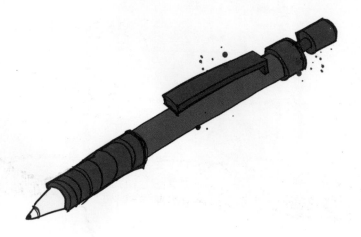

Contents

CHAPTER ONE

'What are you going to do today?' said Aunt Fanny to **the Five.**

They all looked up from their books – except Timmy, who looked up from the bone he was gnawing.

'We ought to go for a walk, I suppose,' said Julian. 'But the wind's so bitter today. I always think January is a pretty dreary month, unless there's snow – or we can go skating.'

'But there's no snow, and no ice – only this horrible, freezing wind,' said Anne. 'I'd just as soon stay in and **read** my **Christmas books!**'

'Oh no – we *must* go out,' said George at once. 'What about Timmy? He's got to have his usual walk.'

Timmy's ears pricked up at once when he heard that word. **Walk!** *Ha* – just what he **was wanting!** He got up at once and ran to George, whining.

She patted him. 'All right, all right, Tim – we'll leave Anne here with her books, and we'll go out for a nice long walk.'

'Would you like to go to **the cinema** in **Beckton**?' asked her mother. 'There's a good film on today, about circus life. I'll pay for you all, if you'd like to go this afternoon.'

'**Mum** – I think you're trying to get **rid of us!**' said George.

'Well – in a way I am,' said her mother, with a laugh. 'Your dad has two friends coming to see him this afternoon – and I really think it would be easier if you were out of the house.'

'Oh, I *see*,' said George. 'Two more of his scientist friends, I suppose. Well, I'd just as soon be out in that case. It's awful not even to be able to sneeze in case I get into trouble for making a noise.'

'Don't exaggerate, George,' said her mother. 'Well, Julian – would *you* like to go to the cinema?'

'Of course – and it's very kind of you to pay for us,' said Julian. 'I tell you what – we'll **walk** to **Beckton,** so that we'll give our legs a stretch – and get the **train** back.'

'Yes. That's a good idea,' said Dick. 'I feel as if I want a good run. Just listen to Tim thumping his tail on the ground. He thoroughly agrees!'

CHAPTER TWO.

So that afternoon, **the Five** set off to **walk** to **Beckton.** The wind was in their faces, and it was very cold indeed; but they were soon warm with walking, and even Anne began to enjoy striding out against the wind.

Timmy loved it, of course. He was full of high spirits, and pranced and capered and bounded about joyfully. He wagged his long tail nineteen to the dozen, chased dead leaves as if they were rats, and made everyone laugh at him.

'Dear Tim,' said Anne. 'It must be lovely to be a dog, and have **four legs** to leap about on, instead of **just two!'**

Halfway to Beckton they came to a big, rather **lonely-looking house** called **Tarleys Mount.** The gates opened on to a short drive that ran to the front steps of the house. On the top of one of the stone gateposts sat a **BIG black cat.** It looked disdainfully down at Timmy.

At first Timmy didn't see it, and then he suddenly caught sight of it and stopped. A **cat!** And a big one, too. But sadly, *just* **out of reach!**

Timmy pranced in front of the gatepost and barked loudly. The cat yawned widely, and then began to wash one of her paws, as if to say – *'A dog! Nasty smelly creature! Not worth taking notice of!'*

But Timmy could leap very high, and the cat was suddenly startled to see his head appearing near the top of the gatepost as he jumped. She hissed and spat.

'Stop it, Timmy,' said George. 'You know you're **not allowed** to **chase cats. Come here!'**

17

The cat spat again. That was too much for Timmy, and he jumped so high that the cat was really alarmed. She leapt right off the gatepost, and shot into the bushes at the side of the drive.

Timmy was **after her** in a flash, yelping madly.

George yelled, but he took no notice at all.

'**Bad dog,**' said Julian. 'He'll be ages chasing that cat and hunting for it. He ought to know by now that he **isn't a match** for **any cat living!**'

'I'll go in and see if I can get him,' said George. 'Hope I don't meet an **angry gardener!**'

'We'll come with you,' said Dick. 'Come on. I can hear Tim down the drive. He must be near the house.'

CHAPTER THREE

They went in at the gate and down the little drive. Yes – Timmy was by the front door, barking under a tree there.

'I bet the cat's sitting on a branch making faces at him,' said Julian. 'Call him, George.'

'Timmy, **Timmy!** Come here **at once!**' shouted George. But he wouldn't.

Then just as they got up to him and George was bending down to take hold of his collar, the cat leapt down the tree and raced round the house to the back. Timmy was after her at once, yelping madly.

'**Oh *no!*** said George, vexed. 'We'll have the people of the house out after us – they must wonder what's going on!'

They ran round the house after Timmy, and came to the back entrance. There was a little yard there, with a clothes line and two or three dustbins and a coal bunker. The cat was now sitting on top of the bunker, daring Timmy to leap up and get her.

'Now then, you dog – you **leave** that **cat alone!'** said an angry voice as the four children turned into the yard. They saw a neat little woman standing there, in a thick coat with a scarf round her head. She held a small basket in her hand, with a little bottle of milk in it and a jar.

'I'm so sorry about our dog,' said George, and pounced on Timmy. She got hold of his collar this time and spoke to him sharply. **'I'm ashamed of you! Bad dog! Very bad dog.'**

Timmy's tail drooped, and he gave George's hand a very small lick. The little woman watched him, frowning.

'He gave me a real fright, that dog of yours,' she said. 'Tearing into the yard like a mad thing – first **old Sooty** the **cat** – then the **dog!'**

'I hope his barking didn't disturb the people in the house,' said Julian.

'What's that you say?' said the woman, cupping her hand behind her ear. **'I'm a bit deaf.'**

'I SAID I HOPE HIS BARKING DIDN'T DISTURB THE PEOPLE IN THE HOUSE,' repeated Julian in a louder voice.

'Oh, **they're away,**' said the little woman, taking off the top of the milk bottle. 'Miss Ella went on Monday, and her **old aunt** went **yesterday.** I just came to feed the old cat. Here, Sooty – come and lap your milk, and I'll put your fish down, too. Hold that dog, please.'

She emptied some cooked fish out of the jar, and poured milk into an enamel saucer by the back doorstep. The cat sat on the coal bunker and looked down longingly, but wouldn't come near it.

'WE'LL TAKE THE DOG AND GO,'
said Dick.

'What did you say?' said the woman.
'Oh yes – you go; then old Sooty will come
along down. He must be hungry.'

CHAPTER FOUR

The four children went round the house again,
George holding Timmy's collar.

'Funny – I can **hear somebody talking!**' said Anne, suddenly, as they
went along the drive. 'Can you, Dick?'

'Yes,' said Dick, puzzled. 'But there's
nobody about.'

They all stopped to listen. 'It sounds like
a **loud conversation**,' said Julian. 'Is it coming
from the house?'

'No – you heard what the woman said. **The people are away,'** said George. 'It must be somebody talking very loudly in the road.'

But the talking **couldn't** be heard when they reached the gates. 'Oh well – it was probably gardeners somewhere in the trees off the drive,' said Dick. 'Come on – we'll be late for the film, if we don't hurry up.'

They were just in time
for it and settled down to watch
the circus story on the screen. It was
very good, and they all enjoyed it thoroughly.

They collected Timmy from the kindly attendant, and he barked in welcome.

They felt very hungry, and the little café opposite looked very inviting, with its wonderful display of cakes in the window.

'Come on – **I'll buy tea for everyone** – providing George doesn't **eat** more than **six cakes!**' said Julian, rattling the money in his pocket. 'Timmy, I'll buy you one too.'

They had a wonderful tea, and finished
up with an ice-cream each. Timmy was treated
to a cake and a biscuit, and licked George's ice-
cream saucer clean.

'Well – I don't know if we can *manage* to walk to the station now!' said Dick. 'I feel pretty full. What's the matter, George?'

'I was just feeling Timmy's collar – and he's **lost** his Tail Wagger badge,' said George. 'It's got his name and address on it. **Oh no!** I only bought him a **new one** last week.'

'If we want to catch the train back, we'd better get a move on,' said Julian, looking at his watch.

CHAPTER FIVE

'No, I'm going to **walk** home,' said George. 'I've got a torch. I may **find Timmy's badge.**'

'Oh, for pity's sake!' groaned Dick. 'Don't say we've got to walk back hunting for the badge all the way home. No, George – that's too much.'

'I can go alone, with Timmy,' said George. 'I didn't mean you others to come.'

'Well – we can't let you walk a mile or two home in the dark by yourself,' said Julian. 'I tell you what – I'll go with *you,* George, and Dick and Anne can go back by train.'

'No, thanks,' said Anne. 'I'll come too. I think I know where Tim **dropped his badge. In the drive** of that **big house!** Do you remember when the cat sat up in a tree and Timmy leapt up at her? Well, he caught his collar on a bough – and I bet that's when he lost his Tail Wagger **badge.'**

'Yes – I expect you're right,' said George. 'Timmy's being a bit of a nuisance today – aren't you, Tim? I hope that cat won't be anywhere about in the garden.'

'Tie a bit of string to Tim's collar,' said Dick, producing a piece. 'And **hang on to him, George!** Well – are we ready?'

They all set off in the starry night. They hardly needed their torches once they had got used to the dark, because the stars were so very bright.

They came at last to **Tarleys Mount,** and stopped at the gates.

'Here we are,' said Dick, flashing his torch. 'We know where Timmy went this morning, and if we hunt about we're pretty certain to find the badge.'

'Now, you keep by me, Tim,' said George, holding tightly to the string lead.

They all went down the drive – and in the middle of it they stopped in surprise.

'**I can hear** those **voices** *again* – well, **different ones** this time – **but** *voices!*' said Anne, astonished. 'Who can be out here, talking and talking in the night?'

'**Beats me!**' said Dick. 'Come on – let's go to **that tree** by the **front door**. I bet **the badge will be there!**'

They went to the big door, **still hearing the voices** somewhere away in the distance. Anne suddenly gave a cry, and bent down. '**Yes – here's the badge,** just where I thought it might be. Isn't that lucky?'

'**Oh good!**' said George, and fixed it on Timmy's collar.

'There's somebody *singing* now,' said Dick, standing still and listening. 'It's really odd.'

CHAPTER SIX

'Perhaps it's **a radio** somewhere,' said Anne.
'It sounds a bit like one.'

'But there's no other house near here,'
said Julian. 'Not near enough for us to hear the
radio, anyway.'

The **singing voice stopped** – and **band
music** came **on the air. 'There!'** said Anne.
'That's **the radio all right!** There
can't be any band playing in the open air this
cold night.'

'You're right,' said Julian, puzzled. 'Do you think that the sounds can be coming from **this** house – **Tarleys Mount?'**

'But we know there's no one *there,'* said Dick. 'That woman who fed the cat this morning told us the house was empty. That's why she had to come and feed the cat. And if someone had left the radio on in the house, she'd have heard it and switched it off.'

'No, she wouldn't,' said George.

'Why not?' asked Dick, surprised.

'Well, because **she was *deaf!'*** said George. 'She kept putting her hand behind her ear, don't you remember? *I* think the **radio is on** in the house.'

'You don't think somebody's got in, and is having a good time there – eating what's left in the larder, sleeping in the beds, and listening to the radio, do you?' said Anne.

'It's a bit puzzling,' said Julian. 'I can't imagine anyone going away and leaving the radio *full* on – and it must be, if we can hear it out here. Perhaps we ought to look round a bit. The noise seems to come from over there – the other side of the house, not where the yard is. Let's go round there.'

There was a sudden hiss from a nearby bush, and Timmy pricked up his ears. **That cat** again!

'Hang on to Tim – there's the cat,' said Julian, as a black streak fled across the beam of his torch. 'Come on, now – let's go round the other side of the house.'

As soon as they turned the corner, they came to a terrace, with steps leading down to a garden only faintly to be seen in the starlight. The band music was **suddenly louder** there. There was now no doubt at all that it was **radio music.**

'Well – it's certainly **coming** from the **house,**' said Julian. 'But from **which** room? As far as I can see, the whole place is in **darkness!**'

CHAPTER SEVEN

So it was! Not a chink of light showed anywhere. Julian shone his torch on to each window. They were all tightly shut, as if the house were indeed empty and deserted.

'There's a **tree** that reaches up to that **balcony,'** said Dick. 'I'll shin up and get on to it, and see if I can spot anything in the house. If the curtains aren't drawn there, I can **shine** my **torch in.'**

Up the tree he went, the others shining their torches to show him which branches to climb.

At last he was **on the** **balcony,** his own torch now shining brightly. There were glass doors there, and the curtains of the room behind weren't drawn across the panes. Dick shone his torch through the glass.

'The **radio's** in **this room,** I'm **sure!**' he cried. 'I can hear it clearly. It's on full, too – the noise is coming through a ventilator, above the glass doors! **Oh!**'

'What? **What is it?**' cried everyone, hearing a sudden strange note in Dick's excited voice.

'There's someone in this room!' called back Dick. 'Someone lying on the floor, but I can't see clearly enough. Whoever it is isn't moving at all. I'll tap and see if they hear me.'

The others heard the sound of tapping, and then Dick's voice again. 'Yes – the person moved when I tapped. Who on earth can it be? He must be hurt, I think, but the doors are locked, so I can't get in. I'm coming down again, so shine your torches, will you?'

Dick climbed quickly down the tree, and the others crowded round him excitedly. 'We'll have to get into the house somehow,' said Dick. 'I'm sure it's someone who's hurt – or maybe ill.'

'But how did they get in?' said Julian in wonder. 'And how can we get in, for that matter?'

'We'll try all the doors to begin with,' said Dick. 'Here's a garden door. No, that's locked. Come on round to **the kitchen door.** I suppose that'll be locked, too.'

But it wasn't! It opened easily enough, and the Five trooped into the house, Timmy quite excited.

The noise of the radio suddenly seemed much louder as **they went in.**

'Come on **upstairs,**' said Dick. 'We'll find that **balcony room.** It was all in **darkness,** which made it seem **stranger than ever!**'

They ran up the wide stairs. The sound of the radio was very loud there. They listened intently.

'It's in **that room** over there!'
shouted Dick, and ran to a half-open door. He
shone his torch round, and then let the beam
rest on something lying on the floor. What
could it be?

Julian reached out his hand to the light switch by the door. Click! The light flooded the room and everyone blinked. The radio went on and on all the time, the dance band playing away gaily.

CHAPTER EIGHT

On the floor **near the radio lay a woman.** She looked old and had silvery grey hair. She was dressed in outdoor things, and her hat lay on the floor.

The children looked at her in horror – what *could* have happened?

At last, to their relief, they saw her eyes open, and she looked up at them. Then she tried to speak. 'Water!' she croaked.

George darted out and found a bathroom with glasses. She filled one with water and brought it back. Julian eased the old woman up into a sitting position, and George helped her

to drink the water. She managed to give them a faint smile.

'So silly of me,' she said, in a faraway kind of voice. 'I was just going downstairs to **leave** the **house** by the **back door,** when I **slipped** here on the polished floor. And, and—'

She stopped for a moment, and Anne patted her hand. 'You fell and hurt yourself?' she said. 'Where?'

'I'm afraid it's my hip,' said the old lady. 'I couldn't get up off the floor. I just couldn't. So I wasn't even able to phone for help. And there was **no one in the house** – my niece had gone—'

'And your daily woman **is deaf,** so she **wouldn't hear you call!'** said Julian, remembering.

'Yes, yes,' said the old lady. 'I just managed to get my arm up to **the radio** and **switched it on.'**

'You see, I thought *someone* might hear it – perhaps a policeman coming round the house at night . . .'

'How long have you been lying like this?' asked Anne anxiously.

'Since yesterday afternoon,' said the old lady. 'I just couldn't move, you see. I was glad I had **my outdoor things on** – I'd have frozen stiff last night, it was **so cold!** I was so thirsty, too. Not hungry. Just very, very thirsty.

You dear, **kind children** – oh, I am **so glad to see you!'**

Julian switched off the radio. 'Where's the phone?' he said. 'I'll call for **a doctor – and an ambulance –** and you'll soon be **well cared** for! **Don't you worry!'**

The Five stayed with her until the doctor came and, later on, the ambulance. Then Julian turned out all the lights that had been switched on, and they went into the hall. Julian slammed the front door after them.

'**Come on, Timmy – keep by my side,**' ordered George. '**No more cat-chasing for you!**'

'What's he saying, George?' asked Anne. George chuckled. 'He says, *"Don't talk to me like that, George – if it hadn't been for me chasing that cat today, you'd never have had this little adventure."*'

'Well, Timmy's right, as usual,' said Dick. 'And if chasing a cat leads to saving somebody's life, I'm all for it. **Good old Tim!**'

If you enjoyed this Famous Five short story, there's plenty more action and adventure in the full-length Famous Five novels. Here is a list of all the titles, in the order they were first published.